Wilbur

ie the Witch

Mrs Parmar

Winnie
Spells Trouble!

The Little Ordinaries

The Egyptian

Auntie Aggie

Jerry

For Vetti, a good friend—K.P.
For my lovely friend, Liz Sim—xx

OXFORD
UNIVERSITY PRESS

Great Clarendon Street, Oxford OX2 6DP

Oxford University Press is a department of the University of Oxford.
It furthers the University's objective of excellence in research, scholarship,
and education by publishing worldwide in

Oxford New York

Auckland Cape Town Dar es Salaam Hong Kong Karachi
Kuala Lumpur Madrid Melbourne Mexico City Nairobi
New Delhi Shanghai Taipei Toronto

With offices in

Argentina Austria Brazil Chile Czech Republic France Greece
Guatemala Hungary Italy Japan Poland Portugal Singapore
South Korea Switzerland Thailand Turkey Ukraine Vietnam

Oxford is a registered trade mark of Oxford University Press
in the UK and in certain other countries

British Library Cataloguing in Publication Data
Data available

ISBN: 978-0-19-273668-0 (paperback)

2 4 6 8 10 9 7 5 3 1

Printed in Great Britain

Paper used in the production of this book is a natural, recyclable product
made from wood grown in sustainable forests. The manufacturing process
conforms to the environmental regulations of the country of origin.

Laura Owen and Korky Paul

Winnie
Spells Trouble!

OXFORD
UNIVERSITY PRESS

Contents

Winnie's Double

Winnie Spells Trouble!

Winnie's After School Club

Winnie had spent the morning cleaning the toilets and the bath and her cauldrons and the oven. 'There!' she said as she sat down to munch her lunch. 'I've done the boring things, and now I want an interesting afternoon. What shall we do, Wilbur?'

The calendar was blank. Wilbur was sprawling in the sunshine as flies hummed around his ears. He opened one eye, then closed it again.

'You're as boring as cleaning the toilet!'
Winnie told him. 'Boring, boring, *boring!*'

But just then—**bleepety-bloop!**—
Winnie's mobile moan rang. It was Mrs
Parmar in a tizzy.

'Oh Winnie, I'm desperate!' she said.
'Can you help?'

'Do you want me to do something
pretty with your hair?' said Winnie. 'I've
got some nice spider silk ribbons with
glitter-bug sequins which I could . . .'

'No!' wailed Mrs Parmar. 'Nothing like that! What I need is somebody to run the After School Club. There will be thirteen children with nobody to care for them unless . . .'

'. . . I look after them?' said Winnie.

'Oh, yes! Wilbur and I love playing with little ordinaries. Easy-peasy-caterpillar-squeezy!' Winnie stuffed her mobile moan into her pocket before Mrs Parmar could say anything else. 'Come on, Wilbur, we've got a job to do!'

In the school playground, the thirteen After School Club children were playing nicely. Some were skipping, some were playing with toy ponies, some were climbing the apparatus, and some were looking after dolls.

'I'll only be gone for one hour,' Mrs Parmar told Winnie. Then she held up a finger. 'And you are not—*absolutely not*—allowed to do any magic on the children. Is that understood?'

II

'Understood and undersat,' said Winnie.
'This is going to be as fun as a flea bun!'

Mrs Parmar's car drove away.

'Come on, Wilbur, let's join in!' said
Winnie. Wilbur began juggling with the
footballs.

'Give them back!' shouted the children.

Winnie climbed up the climbing frame,
then hung upside down.

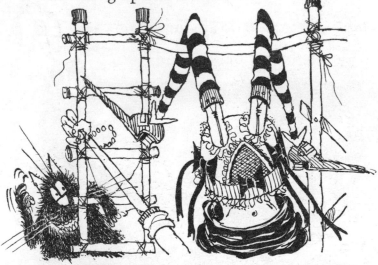

The little ordinaries could see her
bloomers. 'He-ha-hee-hee!' they laughed.
Winnie went red and quickly got down.
Then she jumped onto one end of a seesaw
that had a small boy called Max on the
other end—**clonk-weee-bump!**—
and sent him flying. 'Waah!' wailed Max.
'Whoops!' said Winnie.

'Oi!' said Daisy when Max landed on
her toy ponies.

'Watch what you're doing!' said Charlie
when Daisy toppled backwards and
knocked down his cricket stumps.

'Hey!' shouted the twins when Charlie
slipped and squashed their rocket.

The skippers were tangled in their
ropes. A footballer was hit on the nose by
her ball. Not one child was happy.

'Oh dear!' said Winnie. 'It's all going
wrong-as-boiled-cabbage-pong!'

'Waah!' wailed thirteen little ordinaries.

'What can I do to make it all better?'
wailed Winnie.

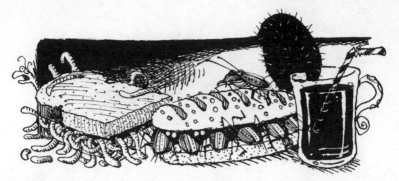

'Meeow?' Wilbur pointed at the picnic basket Winnie had brought with her.

'Good idea, Wilbur. Food always makes things better!' Winnie clapped her hands together. 'Ahem! Shall we all have juice and snacks?' she shouted and for a moment there was silence. 'See?' said Winnie. 'That's much better! Help yourselves, everyone. I've brought fresh worm sandwiches, crunchy cockroach toasties, and cactus cola.'

'Yuck!' complained the little ordinaries and they began wailing again.

Wilbur covered his ears. Winnie wanted to do the same, but she was supposed to be in charge and keeping the children happy! Winnie suddenly knew what to do. She pulled out her wand.

'Mrrro!' Wilbur leapt high to snatch the wand before Winnie could finish waving it.

'But I wasn't going to use magic on the little ordinaries!' Winnie told him. 'Mrs Parmar said I mustn't use magic on them, and I won't. I'm going to use magic on something else!'

Wilbur handed the wand back to Winnie, then braced himself as she waved it wildly over the playground.

18

'Abracadabra!'

Instantly all the toys in the playground came to life. The football was bouncing on its own.

Come on, give us a KICK!

There were real monkeys playing on the climbing frame. 'Ooo, ooo, ooo!'

Baby dolls were gurgling and burping for real.

Tiny ponies galloped past.

The skipping ropes untangled and swung themselves.

For a moment, the little ordinaries were absolutely silent, standing with gawping open mouths. Then somebody said,

'That's magic!'

And suddenly all the children were talking and laughing and cheerfully shrieking and happily shouting.

'Phew!' sighed Winnie. She sat in the sunshine with her hands over her ears.

21

It was not long before Mrs Parmar's car came around the corner and the first of the parents arrived to collect their children.

Up jumped Winnie. She quickly, sneakily waved her wand under the cover of her cardigan.

'*Abradacabra!*' she whispered, to undo her earlier spell. She wasn't sure if Mrs Parmar had heard.

'Has everything been as it should be?' asked a suspicious-looking Mrs Parmar.

'Brillaramaroodles!' said the children before Winnie could answer. 'Mrs. Parmar, please, please, please can Winnie look after us again tomorrow?'

'No!' said Mrs Parmar.

'Not on your smelly-nelly!' said Winnie.

'Mrrr-no!' agreed Wilbur.

Back home, Winnie closed the door and leaned against it.

'Blissaramaroodles!' said Winnie. 'No shouting or screaming. Let's get clean, then have those nice snacks that the little ordinaries didn't eat, and we can watch something magical on television. How does that sound, Wilbur?'

'Meeow,' agreed Wilbur to everything except the bath. He stuck a leg in the air and began to lick himself clean instead.

'Oo, I don't think I'd like to wash myself that way,' said Winnie. 'I'm going to have a nice frogspawn bubble bath, with my little toy duck.

Winnie remembered how happy the little ordinaries had been when their toys came to life. So she waved her wand at the bath water and said, *Abracadabra!* The *real* little duck dived under the water and waggled its fluffy little bottom.

Winnie sank into her bath and giggled at the little duck. But she had forgotten something. Lurking in her bath bubbles was a toy shark.

'Yee-ow!' shrieked Winnie as the *real* little shark took a bite of her big toe.

That was the quickest bath ev
Winnie grabbed her towel in one
and waved her wand in the other—
'Abradacabra!'—to make the shark into a
toy again.

But the frogspawn bubbles from
Winnie's bath weren't wasted. Winnie and
Wilbur enjoyed them as a topping for their
evening hot chocolate.

'Mmm, scrummy!' said Winnie.

28

Winnie
the Naughty Niece

'D'you know what I fancy for lunch, Wilbur?' said Winnie, gazing into the fridge. 'I fancy a simple-as-a-dimple flied egg on toast.'

'Purr!' agreed Wilbur.

Winnie opened the egg box. There were two eggs left: an alligator egg and a boa constrictor egg.

'Now we just need some juicy fresh flies,' said Winnie, 'and then we can get cooking. I know where we'll find flies!'

29

The air over the compost heap hummed hotly with flies and steamily ponged with rotting grass cuttings. Winnie breathed in deeply.

Brrrrm! Jerry, the giant next door, was mowing his lawn. That's where the grass cuttings came from.

'Duck down, Wilbur!' hissed Winnie.
'Don't let Jerry see us or we'll have to invite him for lunch, and we've only got two eggs!'

So they crouched behind the compost heap and tried to catch flies.

'Flapping flip-flops, they're too fast!' said Winnie. 'Oo, I know what would be really good at catching flies.' She waved her wand. *'Abracadabra!'*

And instantly there was a chameleon.

Flick-slurp! Out shot a tongue to lick a fly from the sky. Winnie and Wilbur both jumped because they hadn't seen the green chameleon on the grass cuttings. Its wound-up tongue flipped out to snatch and swallow another fly.

'Oi!' said Winnie. 'You're supposed to be giving the flies to us!' The chameleon spat the next fly into Winnie's hand. And on it went, catching more. Every time, it made Winnie jump.

'Where's that little chameleon gone now?' said Winnie.

Flick-slurp!

Winnie jumped. He was purple, and sitting on Winnie's cardigan.

Flick-slurp!

Now he'd gone blue on Winnie's shoe.

'All this jumping with surprise is making me even hungrier!' said Winnie. 'We've got enough flies now. Let's get cooking!'

But just then there was a shout from Winnie's front door.

'Winifred Isaspell Tabitha Charmaine Hortense, open the door! Your Auntie Aggie is here!'

Gulp! went Winnie. 'Oh no! Hide! Auntie Aggie *can't* stay for lunch because we've only got two eggs! She'll go away if she thinks we're not here.'

But Winnie had forgotten how very
determined Auntie Aggie was. Auntie
Aggie waved her pink plastic wand, and,
Abracadabra! Winnie's front door flew
open, and Auntie Aggie marched into the
house.

'Blooming cheek!' said Winnie. 'Now
what can we do?'

Flick-slurp! Jump! The chameleon was black, hiding in Wilbur's fur.

'That's it! Brillaramaroodles!' said Winnie. 'I know how we can get into the house and cook our flied eggs in the kitchen without Auntie Aggie knowing we're there. Stand still, Wilbur!' Winnie waved her wand. *Abracadabra!*

Instantly both Winnie and Wilbur were covered in sticky treacle.

'Meeow?' asked Wilbur.

'Don't lick it off, Wilbur. It's glue, not food.' Winnie threw herself onto the heap of grass cuttings, and rolled about to cover herself. Wilbur copied her. They looked exactly like two bush shapes—a witchy one and a catty one.

'Now, carefully creep up the path to the door. Auntie Aggie will never guess it's us in disguise!' said Winnie.

Scuttle-scuttle-freeze!
Scuttle-scuttle-freeze! (The freezing in interesting poses happened each time they saw Auntie Aggie looking out of a window.)

Winnie and Wilbur really did look like
bushes because when Scruff from next
door came along he lifted a leg and . . .
'Mrrrow!' hissed the shorter bush.

Winnie and Wilbur went inside, but then they had a problem.

'Er, what is Auntie Aggie going to think if she sees bushes indoors?' wondered Winnie. So she waved a twig, and whispered, *'Abracadabra!'*

Instantly Winnie looked like a tall
lampstand, and Wilbur became a furry
footstool.

They froze when they heard Auntie
Aggie coming into the hall.

'What a ridiculous place to leave a hideous lamp!' sniffed Auntie Aggie. She barged on through the house. 'Winifred, are you in the kitchen?'

'Come on!' hissed the lampstand to the footstool. They scuttled after Auntie Aggie and then froze still because Auntie Aggie suddenly turned and looked at them sharply.

'Hmm,' she said. 'It's so dark and dingy in this miserable house, I shall turn on the light.' She pulled Winnie's necklace.

'Oops!' said the lamp. No light came on.

44

Auntie Aggie frowned and stroked her chin. 'Hmm. This scraggy footstool could do with a good clean. She waved her wand, *Abracadabra!*' suddenly a

pink vacuum cleaner was sucking hard at
Wilbur's fur.

'Mrrrow!' said the footstool in a most
un-footstool-like way. Then the dust being
blown around made the tall lampstand
sneeze in a most un-lampstand-like way.

'Aha, I knew it!' Auntie Aggie clapped
her hands. 'Come out at once, Winifred
and Wilbur!'

So Winnie and Wilbur revealed
themselves. Winnie braced herself ready
for a telling-off.

But Auntie Aggie laughed. 'What a
fun game!' she said. 'Much better than
ordinary hide-and-seek. Give us all some
lunch, Winifred, and then let's play again.'

'B-b-but we were going to have flied
eggs for lunch,' said Winnie. 'And we've
only got *two* eggs!'

'Oh, phooey, what do you think a wand
is for?' said Auntie Aggie. 'Honestly,
you young people these days have no
gumption!' Auntie Aggie waved her pink
plastic wand, and said a very commanding,
'Abracadabra!'

Instantly there was an ostrich egg and a
hummingbird egg and a hen egg and a toad
egg and a crocodile egg.

'The ostrich one is for your big
neighbour who was cutting the grass,' said
Auntie Aggie. 'I invited him to lunch. You
don't mind, do you?'

And Winnie didn't mind now that there was enough food for everyone.

After lunch they all played hide-and-shriek. And none of them noticed the best hider of all who was never found—the chameleon.

Winnie's Double

'Where—**hop**—is my—**hop**—other—
hop, hop—blooming—**hop**—
stocking?' wailed Winnie one morning.

'Meow,' shrugged Wilbur, who didn't
understand problems about clothes. Why
have peel-off warm layers on legs when
you could just be furry all the time?

'My new broom is being delivered in
half an hour. What will the delivery lady
think if I've only got one stocking on?'
Hop, hop!

'Meow?' Wilbur handed Winnie her wand.

'Oo, good idea, that cat!' said Winnie. 'I'll do a times-two spell to get another stocking. Winnie was hop-hopping in front of her mirror, and she waved her wand, once, twice, *Abracadabra!*'

And instantly there were two . . .

. . . Winnies!

'Whoever in the witchy world are *you*?' asked Winnie, gazing at the other Winnie.

'And who the blooming bloomers are *you*?' asked the Mirror Winnie.

'I'm Winnie, of course!' said Winnie.

'Me too. Or two!' shrieked Mirror Winnie. 'Winnie and Winnie!'

'Twins!' shrieked Winnie, and she and
the other Winnie tossed their wands into
the air, held hands, and danced around in a
shriek-giggling witchy circle until Wilbur
couldn't tell which Winnie was 'witch'.

'Mrrow!'

'Wilbur wants his breakfast,' said
Winnie.

'He wants his breakfast, does Wilbur,'
said the other Winnie.

'Meeow!' nodded Wilbur, and then he
purred because one Winnie put down a
bowl full of fish, and one put down a bowl
full of stringy treats.

'Purrr!' Wilbur scoffed a mouthful of
stringy treats.

'But I thought that floppy-flappy fish was your favourite, Wilbur!' wailed one Winnie. 'Don't you like flappy-floppy fish anymore?'

One of the Winnies looked so disappointed that Wilbur spat out the stringy treats, and began to chew the flippy-flappy fish, making appreciative mmm-yum-purr sounds . . . until he saw that the other Winnie was looking upset.

58

'Don't you like the stringy treats,
Wilbur?'

So Wilbur added a stringy treat into
his already full mouth. He looked up
at the two Winnies. Which was the real
Winnie—*his* Winnie? He just couldn't tell!

'Well, what would you like for your breakfast?' one Winnie asked the other.

'I fancy a bowl of spawn flakes topped with yak yogurt and a sprinkling of pong berries,' said the other Winnie.

'Me too, me too!' shrieked the first Winnie. 'With a nice hot cup of . . .'

'. . . ditchwater tea!' shrieked the other Winnie. 'Oo, it's as nice as a lice lolly on a hot day to have a twin who likes exactly the same things that I do!'

They were all still eating breakfast when, **Wiinnniiieee!** shrilled the dooryell.

'My new broom!' shrieked both Winnies at once. Then they scowled.

'It's *my* new broom!' they both said.

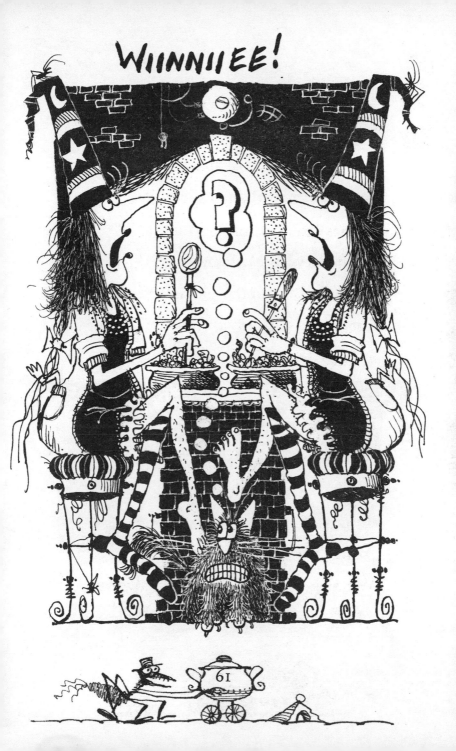

They raced for the door, jamming the opening as they both tried to be the first to go through it.

Wilbur hurried away upstairs to fetch something.

'Delivery for Ms Winnie the Witch,' said the lady with the parcel and the clipboard.

'That's me!' answered both Winnies.

Both Winnies signed the lady's bit of paper, then both Winnies took hold of the broom parcel. They each pulled an end of paper as if it was a giant cracker— **rip!**—and the smart new broom fell onto the floor as both Winnies tried to jump onto it.

'It's only big enough for one,' said one
Winnie. 'And it's my broom! I signed the
paper!'

'So did I!' said the other Winnie. 'And I
blooming ordered it!'

With both Winnies sort-of on board,
the broom wobbled and lurched out of
the house, swooping up . . . and then

stopping still and refusing to go further as
the Winnies tipped it back and forth like a
mid-air seesaw.

'It's mine!'

'No, it's *mine!*'

Wilbur came out just in time to see the
broom buck like a bronco, and toss both
the Winnies—**whee-splosh!**—into the

pond—**splash-splutter!**

'Mee-he-hee!' laughed Wilbur as
two Winnies squelched out of the mud,
dripping with wet and slime and pondy
creatures.

'Being a twin is as much fun as knitting
with jelly. I'm going to magic you *gone!*'
said one Winnie.

'Not before I've magicked *you* gone!'
said the other.

Both Winnies reached into their pockets for their wands. And both found those

pockets empty. Only Wilbur had a wand that he'd fetched from upstairs. There was now only one wand.

'Give it to me, Wilbur! Then we can go back to being just you and me again, like two happy maggots in an apple,' said one Winnie.

Ah, that's definitely my real Winnie, thought Wilbur. He was about to hand her the wand . . .

'Wilbur! She's just the mirror one. I'm the real *me!* Can't you tell?'

'Meow!' Wilbur shook his head, because he really couldn't.

'Remember the time when you were a kitten, and you fell into the cauldron and turned into a purple newt?'

'Meow,' smiled Wilbur, who *did* remember, and he was about to hand the wand to that Winnie when . . .

'Wilbur, I'm the only one who knows where you like to be tickled best, behind your left ear,' said the other Winnie.

'Meow!' said Wilbur, because that, too, was true.

'Give me the wand, Wilbur!' said both Winnies, and poor Wilbur felt totally torn. Then he noticed something. One Winnie had a stocking on her left leg, and the other had a stocking on her right leg. That was their only difference. But which leg had *real* Winnie had her stocking on this morning?

Wilbur thought really hard. *His* Winnie had been hopping on her *right* foot, with her *left* leg bare. So Wilbur let *that* Winnie

snatch the wand from his paw.

'Thank you, clever old Wilbur!' said real
Winnie.

'But it's *mine!*' protested the other.

Real Winnie waved the wand anti-
clockwise, and shouted,
'Abracadabra!'

And instantly the other Winnie was
gone. All that was left was a puddle where
she had been standing. There was peace
and quiet except for the sound of pond
water drip-dripping from real Winnie.

72

'Well, thank fish fingers she's gone!'
said Winnie. She wriggled her bare toes on
her left foot. 'And I'll tell you something
for nothing, Wilbur. I've decided that I
don't care a flea's burp that one leg's got a
stocking on it, and the other hasn't. Why
should legs be both the same? I've gone
off things being just the same. And what's
wrong with being as scruffy as a scrubbing
brush, anyway?'

'Meeow,' agreed Wilbur.

73

Winnie
Spells Trouble!

'Up you get, Wilbur!' Winnie prodded her wand into the ball of black fuzz that was Wilbur.

'Meow!' scowled Wilbur. He'd been in the middle of a lovely dream about mice and bobble hats and fish cakes.

'Hurry up!' bossed Winnie. 'Mrs Parmar says that the teacher has tripped over the caretaker and been taken off to hospital, so they need another grown-up for taking the little ordinaries to the

museum. It'll be as fun as dipping your ice cream into fish bait, Wilbur! Come on!'

The children walked from school to the museum, two by two, holding hands.

'I'll hold hands with you, Mrs Parmar,' said Winnie.

'You will *not!*' said Mrs Parmar, crossing her arms. So Winnie held paws with Wilbur instead.

They walked into the echoey cool
museum full of strange things with labels
and musty smells.

'We are to *do* the Egyptians,' said Mrs
Parmar, leading them into a room full of
mummies and pottery and jewellery and
tools. 'Winnie, please read out what it
says on the label beside that carved stone
coffin. It's called a sarcophagus. Listen to
Winnie, children!'

But Winnie couldn't read hard words
like 'sarcophagus', and the children and
Mrs Parmar were waiting.

'Er,' began Winnie, 'Er . . .' Then,
luckily,

'Oo-ooo-oooo!' One boy was jigging
up and down, red in the face.

'What is it, Henry?' asked Mrs Parmar.

'I need to go to the loo-ooo-oooo!' said
Henry. 'I really really do-ooo-oooo!'

Winnie couldn't read words well, but she could read pictures.

'There's what you want!' she said, pointing to a pair of doors, one with a picture of a lady on it, and one with a picture of a man.

'Come along then, Henry,' said Mrs
Parmar. 'Winnie, you are to stay here
with the other children, and *don't go
anywhere!*'

'Look!' said Daisy. 'There's a cat, all
wrapped tight in bandages! Shall we wrap
up Wil. . .'

Wilbur quickly hid behind Winnie's

legs. But Winnie was looking closely at
the sarcophagus. As well as a lady's face
painted on it, there were lots and lots
of little pictures of birds and hands and
beetles and triangles.

'That's writing in pictures!' said Winnie.
'I can read that!'

'What does it say, then?' asked the
children.

'Well,' said Winnie. She pointed her
wand at a particular little picture, and ...
kerpooof!

The museum seemed to melt and swirl
into a rushing wind that turned into a
whirl of sand and heat.

'Wilburrrr!' Winnie clutched Wilbur's
paw as they spun into the time-changing
magic. The children clutched each others'
hands too, and one held on to Wilbur's tail

so that they all flew like the tail of a kite
from the present day, back through time
to . . .

'Phew, it's as hot as dragon's hanky
when he's blown his nose!' said Winnie,
landing in a flat desert kind of a place.

'Meeow!' said Wilbur, pointing at
Winnie because she suddenly looked like
an Egyptian queen.

Winnie wasn't the only one looking
different. She pointed at Wilbur.

'You're as smart as a mouse tart,
Wilbur!'

And all the children were wearing rags!

Some of the slave children brought
Winnie a throne. One of them fanned her
while others played music.

'Ooo, I like this!' said Winnie.

Wilbur was happy too. Child slaves were
bringing him treats to eat, and they were
down on their knees, crawling before him.

'Ooo, Wilbur, they're worshipping
you!' laughed Winnie.

But Wilbur gave her such a powerful look that Winnie quickly stopped laughing. 'Er, I mean your great cattiness, oh wonderful and wise Wilbur.'

'Meow,' nodded Wilbur.

'Thank you, thank you, you little ordinaries!' said Winnie.

But when Winnie sat back on her throne she noticed that most of the children were being shouted at by a man with a whip. The poor children were heaving on a rope to pull a huge stone. They were sweating and panting.

'Oi!' shouted Winnie to the man. 'Leave those little ordinaries alone! Don't be such a bully!' But the man didn't seem to understand English.

'Oh, heck in a handbag, I'd better get
them safely back to the museum before
Mrs Parmar notices we've gone,' said
Winnie. 'But that man isn't going to let
them go until the job is finished, so . . .'
Winnie waved her wand.

Abracadabra!

In a blur of speed, with super-human strength, the children picked up the huge stones, ran to the half-built pyramid and added the stones to the triangular walls clomp, clonk, clunk! It wasn't the most perfect pyramid in the history of ancient Egypt, but the children finished the job in supersonic time. The man with the whip just stood with his mouth open.

'Come along, all you little ordinaries,
you're all free!' shouted Winnie. 'Now we
just need Wilbur.'

But Wilbur wasn't keen to leave.

'Mrrro,' said Wilbur, shaking his head.
Being worshipped was nice!

'I'll serve you treats when we get home,'
said Winnie. Wilbur gave her a look.

'I *might* even do it on my hands and knees,' said Winnie. Wilbur couldn't see that she had her fingers crossed behind her back. 'Now, everybody hold hands and paws!'

Winnie waved her wand. *'Abracadabra!'*

In a whirl of time and space and sand
they were all dropped back into the
museum at the feet of Mrs Parmar.

'*Winnie the Witch, you promised . . . !*'
began Mrs Parmar. But then one of the

children began plucking the ancient
Egyptian harp she had brought back, and
another rattled a thing that looked like a
potato peeler. Suddenly there was twangy
music filling the echoey museum. The
effect on Mrs Parmar was as instant as

magic. She began to move like an ancient Egyptian, arms and hands bent at angles.

'Walk this way!' said Mrs Parmar, jerking along. So they all *did* walk that way, in single file out of the museum, and all the way back to school . . . where they found the teacher back from hospital,

wrapped in bandages, and looking like a mummy. He made them all write about ancient Egypt. Winnie wrote too, but she did hers in picture-writing.

Back home, Winnie fed nice crunchy beetles to Wilbur. And he fell asleep, dreaming of mice and camels and pyramids, and everyone worshipping him. Purrrr!

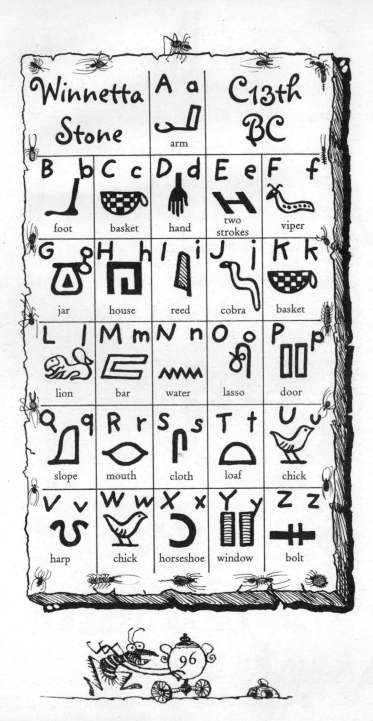

Winnetta Stone A a C13th BC

A a — arm

B b — foot
C c — basket
D d — hand
E e — two strokes
F f — viper

G g — jar
H h — house
I i — reed
J j — cobra
K k — basket

L l — lion
M m — bar
N n — water
O o — lasso
P p — door

Q q — slope
R r — mouth
S s — cloth
T t — loaf
U u — chick

V v — harp
W w — chick
X x — horseshoe
Y y — window
Z z — bolt